The Dream Mouse

Also by Barbara Juster Esbensen

The Dream Mouse

A Lullaby Tale from Old Latvia

by Barbara Juster Esbensen   Illustrated by Judith Mitchell

Little, Brown and Company

Boston   New York   Toronto   London

Acknowledgments

This book owes its existence to the Latvian writer Vitauts Lūdens. Although
we met only briefly when he visited the United States, he urged me to write
a children's book based on the ancient Latvian *daina*s. My thanks to him for his
generous gifts of translations, museum photographs, and the moving history
behind the collecting of these folk songs.
My thanks also to the Kerlan Library, University of Minnesota, for introducing us.

B. J. E.

First Edition

Library of Congress Cataloging-in-Publication Data

Esbensen, Barbara Juster.
    The Dream Mouse : a lullaby tale from Old Latvia / Barbara Juster Esbensen : illustrated by
Judith Mitchell. — 1st ed.
    p. cm.
    Summary: The Dream Mouse drives his cart with its load of sleep through the darkening village,
bringing wondrous dreams to all the children.
    ISBN 0-316-24975-0
    [1. Dreams — Fiction. 2. Sleep — Fiction. 3. Night — Fiction. 4. Mice — Fiction.] I. Mitchell,
Judith, 1951– ill. II. Title.
PZ7.E7446Dr 1995
[E] — dc20   91-18164

10 9 8 7 6 5 4 3 2 1

NIL

Published simultaneously in Canada
by Little, Brown & Company (Canada) Limited
and in Great Britain by Little, Brown and Company (UK) Limited

Printed in Italy

For Eulalie C. Beffel (1905–1994)
— my only teacher.
You gave my young words
the courage to fly
and changed my life.
With love, Barbara

❖❖❖❖❖❖❖❖❖

This book is for Chris Paul for her encouragement, guidance, and patience;
for my children of choice —
Christopher, Amanda, Andrew, Alexandra, Trista, and Robert;
and for the late Ms. Edwina, a lovely Vermont Deer Mouse
J. M.

*E*vening is coming over the land, over the green sea. The edge of the sky glows red where the sun spreads her silk skirt in the cool air.

Along the path, the Dream Mouse drives. His cart creaks with its load of sleep.

From every doorway the mothers call out, "Drive into this yard, Mouse. There are many wakeful children here."

The nightingale sings in the birdcherry bush. Aspen leaves tremble in the small wind as the Dream Cart passes.

"Child," the Dream Mouse whispers, "your father returns
from the sea. In your dreams, will you know him?

He wears a coat of shining herring scales and a cap of sea foam.
With every wave, the sea tosses silver coins into your dreams."

"Child, I bring you this dream of a white swan. Out on the still lake she swims in a snowy shirt, whiter than linen.

Even your big sister, beating the flax all day, cannot make linen as white as this."

"Child, you will dream of the wedding day when the sun's daughter wore a circle of flowers in her long golden hair.

She married the moon in his starry cloak. And she hung her wreath on the low branch of an oak tree."

Along the path, the Dream Mouse drives. His cart creaks with its load of sleep.

He passes the village pump. Clear water gushes where marsh marigolds hold open their cups in the last light of day.

"Child," he whispers, "dream of the river where the otter rests, wearing golden shoes.

Dream of the river singing to itself, ringing against the stones, sifting silver."

◇❖◇❖◇❖◇❖◇❖◇

Listen, child! Do you know Father Thunder? He has nine sons. Three strike. Three rumble. Three flash lightning.

◇⬧◇⬧◇⬧◇⬧◇⬧◇⬧◇

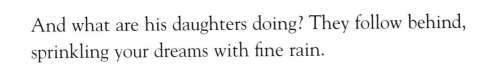

And what are his daughters doing? They follow behind,
sprinkling your dreams with fine rain.

Bees in the hollow oak have hushed their melodies. Under the steep little roof, the bee in its hive is weaving you a honey dream.

In your dream the bee's waxy candles will wink on one by one in the village windows.

Along the path to your door, the Dream Mouse drives. His cart creaks with its load of sleep. The cradle hangs from its ribbon, rocked by white-footed sheep, and under a flowered tent the baby's eyes are closing.

Are you still awake in your snug little bed? Sleep waits in the doorway, teasing, teasing. Won't it come into the room? Yes! Mother will take her birch-twig broom and sweep it into your cozy bed!

Softly the Dream Mouse drives away from your door. The sky is drenched with starlight. Even the flat-footed bear cubs slumber. They send you a dream of honey and berries.

Hush, child, your sweet dreams are here.

The Dream Mouse

Velc, pe - lī - te,   sal - du mie - gu   ma - za - ja - mi   bēr - ni - ņam.

(Pull, mouse, sweet sleep for the little child.)

Author's Note

Many of the ideas and images in *The Dream Mouse* were taken from a collection of *dainas*, ancient Latvian folk songs, gathered in the late 1800s by a Latvian scholar, Krisjanis Barons. He sent out word to all parts of his country asking for these oldest of songs. The people of Latvia responded to his call. He received hundreds of thousands of these little four-line folk songs, some dating back hundreds of years. The first of many volumes of Barons's collection, entitled *Latvian Dainas*, was published in 1894.

The anthology I used had 150 songs. I roamed through their lines, finding the word-pictures I could use in this book. Then I used words of my own to tie it all together. I hope that I have given this Dream Mouse with his "load of sleep" a safe journey through the darkening village and that he will reach the sleepy child's own room at last.